SPACE COWS

by Eric Seltzer
illustrated by Tom Disbury

Ready-to-Read

Simon Spotlight

New York   London   Toronto   Sydney   New Delhi

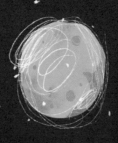

For Irving and Harriet Berg—E. S.

For Toby and Harry—T. D.

SIMON SPOTLIGHT
An imprint of Simon & Schuster Children's Publishing Division
1230 Avenue of the Americas, New York, New York 10020
This Simon Spotlight edition August 2018
Text copyright © 2018 by Eric Seltzer
Illustrations copyright © 2018 by Tom Disbury
SIMON SPOTLIGHT, READY-TO-READ, and colophon are registered
trademarks of Simon & Schuster, Inc.
For information about special discounts for bulk purchases, please contact
Simon & Schuster Special Sales at 1-866-506-1949
or business@simonandschuster.com.
Manufactured in the United States of America 0119 LAK
2 4 6 8 10 9 7 5 3
The book has been cataloged with the Library of Congress.
ISBN 978-1-5344-2876-8 (hc)
ISBN 978-1-5344-2875-1 (pbk)
ISBN 978-1-5344-2877-5 (eBook)

Space cows fly high.

Space cows fly low.

Space cows dance
three in a row.

Some space cows are green.

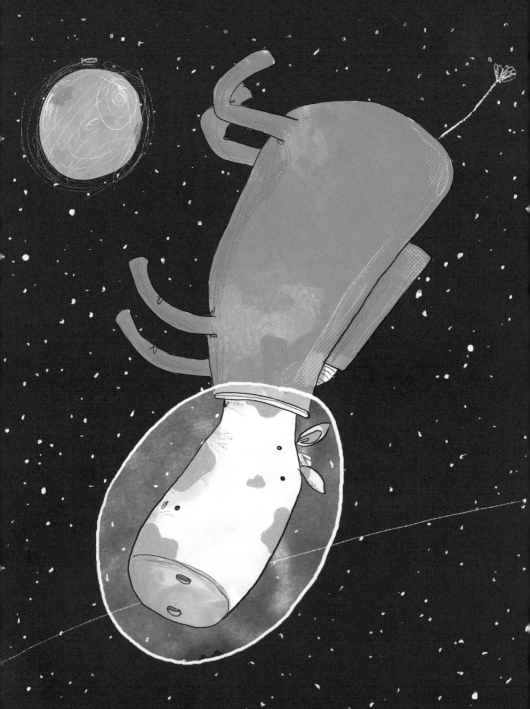

Some space cows
are blue.

Some of them quack . . .

Space cows are big.

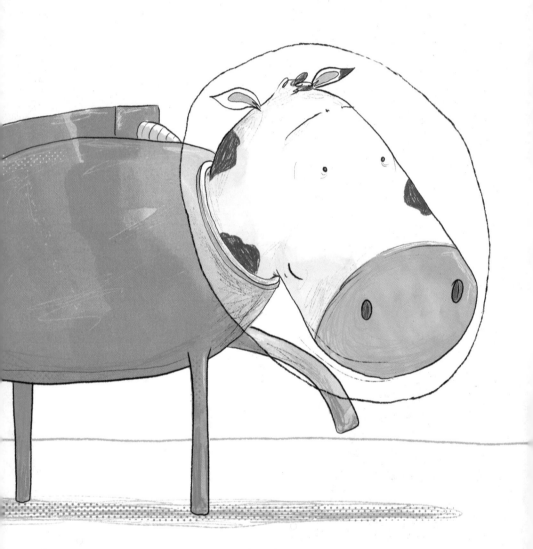

Space cows are tiny.

Most of them
are happy . . .

... but this
one is whiny.

Space cows eat chips
on long space cow trips.

Then space cows sleep
in space cow spaceships.

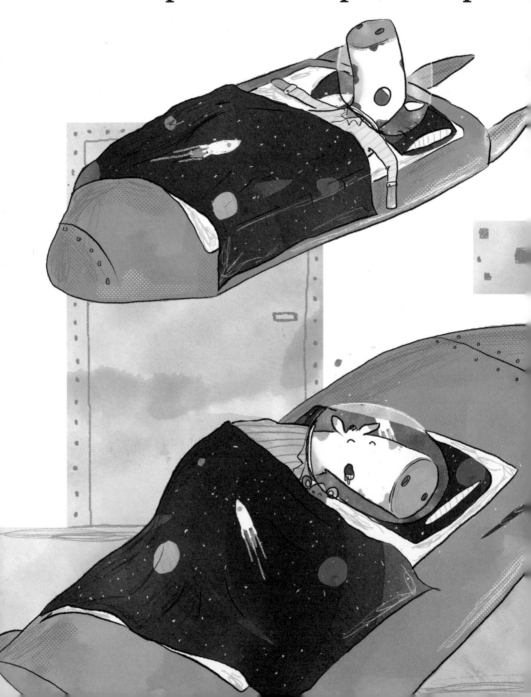

Are there space cow babies?
Yes, there is one!

All he wants is to have space cow fun!

Space cows like games.

Space cows like toys.

Space cows do not like
lots of noise.

They cover up
their space cow ears.

First it is silent. . . .

Then they all cheer!

Now what will these
space cows do?

Space cows are coming to a planet near you!